With a big hug for my friend Rebecca Guay

Who Wants a Hug?
Copyright © 2015 by Jeff Mack
All rights reserved. Manufactured in China.
No part of this book may be used or reproduced in any manner whatsoever without written permission except
in the case of brief quotations embodied in critical articles and reviews. For information address HarperCollins
Children's Books, a division of HarperCollins Publishers, 195 Broadway, New York, NY 10007.
www.harpercollinschildrens.com

Library of Congress Cataloging-in-Publication Data
Mack, Jeff.
    Who wants a hug? / written and illustrated by Jeff Mack. — 1st ed.
        p.   cm.
    Summary: Everyone likes Bear except grouchy Skunk, who devises a plan to make Bear stop being happy and
hugging others.
    ISBN 978-0-06-222026-4 (hardcover bdg.)
    [1. Hugging—Fiction. 2. Bears—Fiction. 3. Skunks—Fiction. 4. Humorous stories.] I. Title.
PZ7.M18973Do 2014   2012022158
[Fic]—dc23   CIP
                                                                                      AC

The artist used ink and pencil on paper and Photoshop to create the digital illustrations for this book.
Typography by Dana Fritts
14 15 16 17 18   SCP   10 9 8 7 6 5 4 3 2 1
❖
First Edition

Who Wants a Hug?

Written and Illustrated by

JEFF MACK

HARPER

An Imprint of HarperCollinsPublishers

Everyone liked Bear.

No one liked Skunk.

"Hello there, Skunk," said Bear.
"Would you like a hug?"

"Why would I want
that?" asked Skunk.

"Because hugs are fun," said Bear.
"They make you feel great!"

"Oh yeah? Well, I'm a skunk, see? . . . And nobody hugs a skunk!"

"It's okay," said Bear.
"I'll save you one for later."

Later . . .

"That bear bugs me," growled Skunk. "He's always happy. He's always hugging. I'll fix him!"

"One smack with this big stinky fish . . .
and Bear will be as huggable as a
thousand-year-old rotten mackerel!"

"Poor Skunk," said Bear.
"You look like you need a hug."

"A SKUNK NEVER HUGS!"
cried Skunk.

"It's okay," said Bear.
"I'll save you one for later."

Later . . .

"This bag of stinky, smelly garbage will stop that bear from hugging," said Skunk.

"I'll hang it from this tree branch, and when he walks under it . . .

. . . POW! He'll be covered in stink!"

"No fair, Bird!" yelled
Skunk. "Let go of my bag!"

So he did.

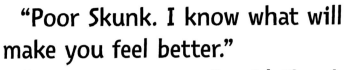

"Poor Skunk. I know what will
make you feel better."
"Let me guess . . ." said Skunk.
"A hug," said Bear.

"Never!" cried Skunk. "How
many times do I have to tell you?
Skunks do not hug!"

"It's okay," said Bear.
"I'll save you one for later."

Later . . .

"That does it!" huffed Skunk.

"There's only one trick left.

A STINK BALLOON!

When this bad boy pops, Bear will smell so bad, no one will ever hug him again."

"I need a rest," said Bear.

Ha!Ha! Ha!Ha!

"I think I'll sit right here."

3 . . . 2 . . . 1 . . .

"Ahh . . ." said Bear.

"Well, I'd better
get back to work."

"What?" cried Skunk.
"Why didn't it pop?"

"No fair! It was supposed to . . ."

Skunk was toast.

"No!" cried Skunk.
"Bear wins again!

"I give up."

"Poor Skunk," said Bear. "You look sad. Would you like that hug now?"

"Oh, fine. I guess I'll have a tiny one."

PU!

"Wow!" said Skunk.
"That was great!"

"It was?"
said Bear.

Later . . .

"Ahh . . ."
said Skunk.